Famous Tales

AKBAR
&
BIRBAL

TM
APPLE
BOOKS

Famous Tales Of
AKBAR & BIRBAL
ISBN 81-7904-051-8 .

© Publishers

This edition published by .
Apple Publishing International (P) Ltd
V-5 (New No.71) 4th Main Road
Anna Nagar, Chennai - 600 040 (India)
Ph : 26224690 Tele Fax : 91-44-26211085
E-mail : info@applebooks.org
Website : www.applebooks.org

Printed in India by Chennai Microprint (P) Ltd.

• CONTENTS •

The Dream	5
One Thought For All	9
The Biggest Fool	13
Justice Done	19
The Wicked Barber	23
Birbal To The Rescue	29
The Emperor's Parrot	35
Who Is Unlucky?	39
The Shorter Line	43
Truth And Falsehood	47
The Poet's Reward	49
New Moon Or Full Moon	55
The Young Prince	59
The Poor Trader	63
Giving And Taking	67
The Impossible	69
Wisdom In A Pitcher	73
The Magic Sticks	77

• CONTENTS •

The Naughty Child	81
The Clever Sadhu	85
The Loyal Birbal	91
Warmth Of The Light	95
Birbal Is Banished	101
The Witness	105
How Many Pigeons	109
Birbal, The Father	113
The Camel's Curved Neck	115
Birbal Frees The Lion	119
Divine Music	121
Clever Birbal	125

The Dream

It was the reign of Akbar the Great. One fine morning the court was in session as usual but the great emperor was not his usual cheerful self. He looked worried and tired. All the courtiers looked at their king and wondered what had gone wrong. The king then called for his astrologer and told him he had not slept well since he had dreamt that he had lost all his teeth except for one tooth.

"Can you tell me what my dream means?" he asked the astrologer. The astrologer looked sadly at the king and

said, "My Lord, it means that all your relatives will die before you die." Akbar was very disheartened when he heard this explanation. He ordered the astrologer to go away and sat pensively on his throne.

Soon his chief courtier, the wise Birbal came to the court. On seeing the emperor look so worried Birbal asked him what was wrong. King Akbar then narrated the strange dream that had so troubled him and asked Birbal if he knew what the dream signified.

"Your Majesty what your dream signifies is that you will live longer than all your kith and kin" replied Birbal. The emperor was very happy to hear that he would outlive all his dear ones and rewarded Birbal for his explanation.

The court astrologer had also listened to Birbal's explanation. He realised that Birbal had given the same explanation that he had given but had said it in a way that would please the emperor. "Now I understand the value of saying things the right way" he thought to himself as he congratulated Birbal on his clever use of words.

One Thought For All

Akbar the Great was known for asking tricky questions which confused his poor courtiers. One evening a story teller was invited to the royal court and was asked to narrate an interesting story for the king's pleasure. As the great emperor sat listening to the story a thought suddenly struck him.

"I wonder what all my courtiers are thinking at this very moment," he thought to himself. Soon the story teller finished the story he had been narrating. The king rewarded him with a bag full of gold coins and sent him on his

way. He then looked at his courtiers and asked: "I would like to know what, all of you courtiers are thinking at this very moment?"

The courtiers looked at each other and wondered how to answer their majesty's question, for how could one person know what the other was thinking. They remained silent and hoped that Birbal would come up with the right answer to the king's unusual question.

Birbal knew that the courtiers expected him to answer for them all. He thought for a moment and then said: "Your Highness, at this very moment all the courtiers including myself are praying to the Lord to give you a very long and prosperous life".

"How do you know that all the courtiers are thinking that very same thought?" asked the king. Birbal pointed to the courtiers and replied, "My lord, why don't you ask them if they had thought of the same thing?" The courtiers by now had realised that if they said they had not thought of the same thing the king would think that they did not wish him well. So they all shook their heads and agreed that they had all been thinking of that very same thought!

Akbar too had by now understood Birbal's clever answer and praised him for his quick wit.

The Biggest Fool

Emperor Akbar was very fond of horses. He had a huge stable which housed a number of fine horses. Collecting horses was one of the emperor's greatest passions. He would often go to his stable and admire his large collection of horses.

One day a trader came to see the emperor and told him that he had with him a few horses which were of a good pedigree. Emperor Akbar asked the merchant to show him the horses the very same day. On seeing the

horses the emperor was very impressed and informed the merchant that he would buy all the horses. He then paid the merchant for the horses. The merchant thanked the emperor and was about to take his leave when the emperor handed him a big bag full of gold coins and said: "Keep these gold coins and bring me a few more fine horses". The merchant took the bag and promised to bring some good horses.

A week later Akbar and his wise minister Birbal were taking a stroll along the palace garden. They were discussing the foolish ways of some people when Akbar asked Birbal to make him a list of all the foolish people he had met.

The next day Birbal handed over the list to the emperor. On taking a look at the list the emperor became very angry for his name was on the top of the list. "Are you saying that I am the biggest fool that you have met so far?" he asked Birbal.

"Forgive my impudence your majesty, but did you not give a total stranger a bag full of gold coins and ask him to buy you some horses?" replied Birbal. The king agreed that he had done so but said that the merchant would return in a few days with the horses. Birbal looked at the king and said, "The day the merchant brings you the horses I will strike off your name from the list".

A few months went by and still there was no sign of the merchant. Since Akbar did not know any details about the merchant he could not even trace him. He then realised what a foolish mistake he had made in trusting a total stranger and agreed that he had been the biggest fool!

Justice Done

One morning Emperor Akbar was in his court attending the morning session when the palace guard suddenly appeared before him, bowed low and said, "Pardon me, Your Highness, there are two women outside the palace gates who insist on seeing you immediately". The king although annoyed with the disturbance, asked the guard to permit the two women into the court.

The two women walked hurriedly into the court and stood before the emperor. It was then that he noticed that one of the women was holding a small child in her arms. "What brings you two women here in such an agitated state?" asked the emperor. "Your Majesty", replied the woman holding the child, "this child which I hold in my arms is my baby". "No, that it is not true" cried the other woman, "My Lord, it is my baby."

The king unable to find a solution asked Birbal to solve the problem and requested him to hand over the child to the rightful mother. Birbal then walked up to the woman with the child in her arms handed her his sword and asked her to cut the child into half so each of the women could take home half of the child.

On seeing the sword and hearing Birbal's words the woman cried out and swooned with shock. Birbal quickly sprinkled some water on her and on reviving her said to the king, "Your majesty, this woman who swooned is the rightful mother of the child, for, it is only a true mother who cannot bear the thought of hurting her child."

So saying Birbal handed over the child to the woman. The woman thanked Birbal profusely and went away happily for justice had been done.

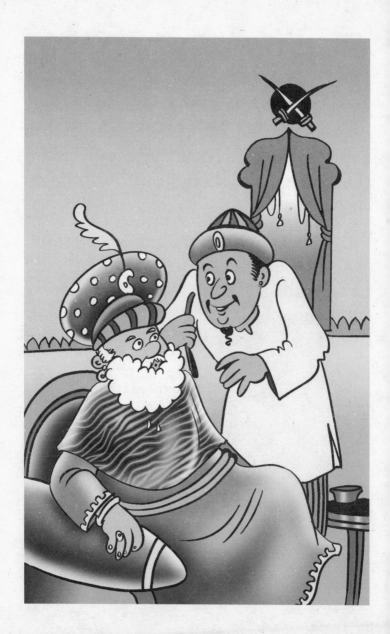

The Wicked Barber

Birbal, because of his wit and sense of fair play had become Emperor Akbar's favourite minister as well as his close companion. Soon many people became envious of the close relationship between the king and Birbal.

One such person was the king's barber who disliked Birbal since the king bestowed all kinds of rewards on him in appreciation of his wise counsel. The barber wanted to somehow get rid of Birbal and soon hit upon a plan.

One day as he was attending to the king the barber said: "Your majesty have you ever thought of how your father the great Emperor Humayun is doing in heaven?" "I too have often wondered about that but how can we find out?" asked the king.

This was the occasion the barber was waiting for. "Your majesty" he said, "I know a person with divine powers who told me how we can send a person to heaven to enquire about our ancestors there." The king was very happy to hear this and asked the barber to explain the procedure. The barber continued: "My friend says that there is an old, unused well which is located near the forest. The man chosen to be sent to heaven must be lowered into that well on a full moon night. He will then be transported to heaven and will return to the well exactly after a month". "But whom can we send?" asked the king.

"The man we send should be a very wise man. Our wise minister Birbal would be the right person for I cannot think of anyone wiser than him", replied the barber. The king approved of this suggestion.

The next day he sent for Birbal and informed him that the barber had come up with a good plan to send him to heaven in order to enquire about his ancestors. The king then explained the entire procedure to Birbal and asked him to prepare for the journey which was to take place on the next full moon night which was only a week away. Birbal concluded immediately that the barber was trying to get rid of him since he knew that the old well contained a lot of poisonous snakes.

That evening Birbal hurried home and called for a few of his trusted men. He then told them to secretly go to the old well and get rid of all the poisonous snakes and to also dig a tunnel from the well to his house. The trusted men soon completed the tasks and were rewarded by Birbal.

On the full moon night Birbal was lowered into the well, with the king and all his men watching him anxiously. Once he had disappeared into the well they all left the place planning to return a month later to receive Birbal on his return from heaven. The barber was especially very happy since he thought that he would never see Birbal again.

Once he reached the bottom of the well, Birbal soon walked through the secret tunnel which led to his house. He hid in his house the entire month during which time he did not cut his hair.

On the expected day of his arrival he walked through the tunnel and back to the old well. He was soon pulled out of the well and was welcomed warmly by the king.

The king then asked Birbal how his ancestors were doing for which Birbal replied: "Your majesty your forefathers are doing well in heaven but the only problem is that they do not have a barber which is why my hair too has not been .cut. They long for a barber and have requested me to send them a good one in two days' time. I cannot think of a better barber than the one who cuts your hair" said Birbal.

The king immediately agreed to the idea and ordered the barber to prepare for the journey.

Birbal then went back home and asked his trusted men to fill the tunnel and close it and to drop some poisonous snakes into the well.

On the second night the king ordered for the barber to be lowered into the well. The barber had no choice as he could not tell the emperor that he had lied about the trip to heaven for then he would surely be beheaded. He then descended the well to meet his dreaded fate knowing fully well that Birbal had outwitted him.

Birbal To The Rescue

Akbar the great had many wives who all stayed with him in his palace. One of them was a quarrelsome woman who often got into disputes because of her sharp tongue.

On one occasion she went too far by quarrelling with the emperor himself. Emperor Akbar in a fit of anger asked her to leave the palace and return to her father's palace.

The queen pleaded with the emperor and promised never to quarrel again. The emperor however would not listen to her and ordered her to

leave the palace by the following day. The poor queen was very disheartened and did not know what to do.

She then thought of Birbal, the wise minister and decided to seek his help. So she went in search of Birbal and told him what had happened. Birbal listened to the queen's story and felt that the emperor had punished her too severely.

He then thought for a minute and asked the queen: "Your Highness, did the emperor say anything else to you after ordering you to go away from the palace?" The queen remained thoughtful for a minute and then replied: "Yes, he did say that I could take with me whatever I liked most from the palace."

Birbal's face lit up when he heard this. He then advised her as to what she should do. Later that evening the queen went up to the king and said: "My lord, I have packed all my belongings and am ready to leave but before I do so, will you please accept this special drink that I have made for you?"

The emperor feeling sorry for the queen drank the drink that she had specially made for him. In a few minutes he fell into a deep sleep.

The next day when the emperor woke up he found himself in a strange room. He called for the queen and asked her where he was. The queen replied, "Please forgive me my lord. You are now in my father's palace. You had told me that I could take whatever I liked most from the palace before I left. It is you that I treasure most. Thus I took you with me when I left the palace".

Emperor Akbar then realised what had happened but instead of punishing the queen he laughed heartily and was happy that the queen loved him so much! He then returned to his own palace with the queen beside him. The queen later thanked Birbal and rewarded him for his timely rescue.

The Emperor's Parrot

Emperor Akbar was once presented with a parrot by a neighbouring king. It was a special parrot for it could talk and sing. The emperor was very impressed with the parrot and soon became very fond of it. He kept the parrot in a beautiful cage made of gold and hired two servants to look after it day and night.

The servants were asked to take special care of the parrot. The emperor had warned them that the one who reported to him that the parrot had died would be put to death.

So the two servants took care to see that the parrot was well kept. As time went by the parrot grew old and died one night.

The servants were in a state of panic when they realised that the parrot had died. They were terrified of conveying the news to the emperor as he had warned them that death would befall them too, if they were to ever tell him that the parrot had died. The two servants finally decided to ask for help from the great minister, Birbal.

On hearing their story, Birbal informed them that he would let the emperor know about the parrot's death. The servants were relieved and thanked Birbal for saving their lives.

Birbal then met the emperor and said to him, "Your majesty, I have witnessed something strange. Your parrot is lying on the floor of it's cage without moving and is not talking or singing. Its eyes are closed and it looks as if it is meditating." "What!" said the emperor "I must go see my precious parrot!". So saying the emperor hurried to see the parrot.

As soon as he saw the parrot lying still in the cage he exclaimed, "Oh no, my poor parrot is dead!" Birbal then looked at the emperor and said, "Your highness, it is you who said that the parrot is dead. It seems that the parrot has grown old and has died a natural death. It was neither your servants nor I who reported it you.

You had warned them that you would put them to death if they ever told you that the parrot had died. Since you said it yourself please spare them your majesty."

On hearing these words the emperor remembered the warning. He felt ashamed that he had foolishly threatened the servants, for what could they do if the parrot had died. He then realised his mistake and thanked Birbal for pointing it out to him.

Who Is Unlucky?

Akbar the Great, once heard a rumour that there was a man in his kingdom who brought bad luck to all those who saw him. Being curious the emperor asked his minister Birbal to arrange for this man to be brought to the palace. He wanted to test if the rumour was indeed true.

So the very next day the man who was known to be unlucky walked into the court and bowed low before the emperor. "So you are the unlucky man", said the emperor, "now that I have seen you, let me see how my day goes". So saying the emperor dismissed the man.

Unfortunately that very day the emperor was very busy and did not have the time to even eat his meals. He had a very difficult and tiring day and by the evening the emperor was mentally and physically exhausted. "Oh what a tough day I've had", he thought.

Suddenly, it struck him that his day had been difficult because he had seen the unlucky man in the morning. "I cannot let such a man who brings bad luck live in my kingdom," he thought to himself. The same evening he called for a meeting and announced that the unlucky man should be put to death.

Birbal who had heard the emperor's order, approached him and said: "Your majesty, that man made you have a bad day since you did not eat the whole day. But what about the poor man? Seeing you first thing in the morning has brought death upon his head! Who do you think is more unlucky?".

Hearing Birbal make this observation the emperor realised how foolish he had been in listening to idle rumour and believing it to be true. He then thanked Birbal for stopping him from doing an injustice to an innocent man.

The Shorter Line

One day Emperor Akbar decided to test the intelligence of all his courtiers. So he called for a meeting to be held in his court.

Once all the courtiers had assembled the emperor got down from his throne and drew a line on the ground with a piece of chalk. "Now", he said to all his courtiers, "I want to see if any one of you can make this line look shorter but without touching it in any way". He then looked up to see all the courtiers looking very perplexed. "Ha!", thought he, "not even my wise minister Birbal can solve this riddle".

No sooner had the emperor thought so, than Birbal took a piece of chalk and drew another longer line below the line the emperor had drawn. "Your majesty, now the line you drew has become shorter compared to the line that I have drawn, is it not so?" asked Birbal with a small smile on his lips.

Emperor Akbar threw back his head and laughed heartily at his favourite minister's cheekiness while admiring his quick wit at the same time.

Truth And Falsehood

One afternoon the emperor Akbar was in a philosophical mood. He called for his best courtier Birbal and asked him, "Tell me Birbal, what is the difference between a truth and a lie?"

Birbal thought for a minute and then promptly replied, "Your highness, the difference between a truth and a lie is the difference between our eyes and our ears." "Can you explain what you just said?" asked the emperor, taken aback with Birbal's answer.

"Yes your majesty. What I meant to say is that what we see with our eyes is the truth and what we hear with our ears is falsehood", said Birbal.

The emperor now understood Birbal's statement and applauded his quick thinking.

The Poet's Reward

In the kingdom of Akbar the Great lived a very wealthy man. Though he was one of the richest men in the entire kingdom, he was known to be a miser.

One day a poet came to him and asked him if he could recite some of the poems he had written. The rich man agreed to listen to his poems. The poet then recited some of his best poems which were indeed very good.

After listening to the poems the rich man said to the poet, "Your poems are indeed very good. I enjoyed listening to them. Please come tomorrow and

collect your reward from me". The poet was very happy to hear this. He went away and promptly returned to the rich man's house the very next day.

"Sir," he said, "I have come to collect the reward you promised to give me today". The rich man looked at the poet and said, "Oh poet, you are a fool. If I had wanted to reward you, I would have done so yesterday. I asked you to come the next day because I did not want to hurt you. Please go away, I have nothing to give you."

The poet who was shocked to hear this left the house feeling very disappointed.

On his way back home he came across Birbal who asked him why he was looking so sad.

The poet then narrated the whole incident to him. Birbal listened to him and then asked the poet: "Do you have a trustworthy friend?" the poet nodded. "Ask your friend to invite the rich man to his house for a feast to be held tomorrow night and then do as I say" instructed Birbal.

So the next day the poet's friend went to the rich man's house and invited him to a feast at his house. The rich man agreed to attend the feast. The next day he eagerly set off to attend the feast at the specified time. When he reached the man's house he found that he was the only person who was there apart from the poet and his friend. The evening went on and they kept talking but there was no sign of any food.

The rich man was very hungry and finally asked the poet's friend when they were going to serve the food. The poet's friend replied, "What food? We did not invite you here for any feast but just for a chat? We have already eaten our dinner earlier this evening and have nothing to give you."

The rich man, on hearing this, understood that they had played a trick on him. He also realised that since he had treated the poet in an unjust manner they had wanted to teach him a lesson. He felt humbled and bad for cheating the poet. He then removed the gold necklace that he was wearing and handed it over to the poet saying that he deserved it for writing such excellent poems.

The poet was happy that he had taught the rich man a lesson, thanks to Birbal's clever plan.

New Moon Or Full Moon

Birbal, along with another minister was once sent to another kingdom as a representative of Emperor Akbar in order to settle an issue.

Birbal paid his respects to the ruling king of the land and said that he had heard many fine things about him. He then commented that the king was like a full moon whereas the ruler of his own land, Emperor Akbar, was like a new moon. The king was happy to hear this and showered Birbal with gifts.

The minister who had accompanied Birbal did not like the comment that Birbal had made. "How could Birbal compare his own emperor to a new moon while comparing the neighbouring land's king to a full moon?" he thought.

On their return the minister promptly repeated Birbal's comment to Emperor Akbar. The emperor was quite upset and asked Birbal to explain what he meant by it.

Birbal looked calmly at the emperor and replied, "My lord, the full moon is the last stage of the moon's growth. It cannot grow any further. Similarly, the other land has grown to it's full extent and will not grow any more. Whereas a new moon keeps growing till it becomes a full moon. Our land too is growing and expanding under your great rule. This is what I meant by making such a comment."

On hearing this, the emperor clapped his hands with gusto and applauded Birbal's wisdom.

The Young Prince

One morning Emperor Akbar returned from his morning stroll in his gardens and went to attend the morning session of the court.

On a sudden impulse he decided to play a prank on his courtiers. He said to them, "This morning as I was returning to the court from my morning stroll in the gardens, someone grabbed my beard and pinched my cheek. I want to know, how I should punish this cheeky fellow?"

The courtiers were shocked to hear of this incident for who would dare to do such a thing to their Highness the emperor of the land? They were very angry with the fellow who had the audacity to manhandle their emperor.

One of the courtiers said: "Your majesty, you should whip this fellow fifty times for what he has done". Another said, "He should be put in jail for the rest of his life." A third said, "He should be hanged."

Emperor Akbar then asked Birbal what he thought was the ideal punishment. "A big hug and lots of kisses, my lord", replied Birbal much to the amazement of all the others. "Explain yourself," said Akbar, to which Birbal replied, "Yes my lord, the culprit deserves what I have just said for who else would have the audacity to manhandle you but your own son, the young prince!"

Emperor Akbar shook his head with approval for Birbal had once again outwitted him!

The Poor Trader

There was once a poor trader in Emperor Akbar's kingdom who made his living by selling a few odd things in his small shop. Opposite his shop was a sweet shop which was owned by a miserly man.

The poor trader would often look at the sweets displayed in the sweet shop and wish he had enough money to buy some. He would also inhale the aroma coming from the shop while having his lunch which made his simple food seem tastier.

One day the owner of the sweet shop saw the trader eating his lunch sitting outside his sweet shop and inhaling the fragrance of all his delicious sweets.

He asked the trader what he was doing. The trader said that the scent of the sweets made his lunch seem tastier, so he liked to eat his lunch outside the sweet shop.

The owner of the sweet shop got angry and demanded that the trader pay for inhaling the delicious smell of his sweets.

The trader refused to do so and both of them decided to take the matter to the emperor's court.

They went to the court and related the incident. Birbal heard the story patiently and said,: "Yes of course the owner of the sweet shop is right. The trader has to pay him for enjoying the aroma of the sweets."

The other courtiers were shocked by Birbal's verdict. Birbal then took out a gold coin and said to the trader: "Please rub this coin on the sweet shop owner's nose and let him get the smell of the coin. By doing so you will be paying him in the same manner that you enjoyed his sweets."

The whole court burst into peals of laughter at Birbal's statement. The shop owner felt ashamed for having unnecessarily harassed the poor trader. He apologised to the trader and the court and left before he was humiliated further by the wise Birbal.

Giving And Taking

It was Emperor Akbar's habit to test the intelligence of his courtiers. He often asked them to solve riddles and rewarded the courtier who came up with the right answer.

One evening he put across a rather puzzling riddle to them. "When one gives a gift his hand is usually on top and the receiver's hand is at the bottom. When is the one time when the receiver's hand is on top?" he asked.

The courtiers thought hard but they could not come up with an answer to this riddle. Just then the emperor's servant brought a small container in a tray and offered it to the emperor. The emperor took a bit of snuff for his nose from the container and sent the servant away. Birbal noticed this and immediately thought of an answer to the puzzle.

"My lord, the one time that the receiver's hand is on top and the giver's below is when he is taking a pinch of snuff for his nose", answered Birbal.

Emperor Akbar knew that Birbal had observed him taking the snuff for his nose. He praised Birbal for being so observant and his quick thinking.

The Impossible

Emperor Akbar once summoned Birbal and asked him to fetch him a pitcher of Ox's milk.

Birbal was very puzzled for he knew that an ox does not produce milk unlike a cow or a goat. He wondered how he was going to do so but promised the emperor that he would bring him the milk within a few days.

Birbal then went back home. At home Birbal's wife noticed that he was looking very disturbed and asked him what the matter was,

"The king has asked me to fetch him a pitcher of ox's milk. How can I do so when an ox does not produce milk," said Birbal with a frown. "Don't worry", said his wife, "for I have a plan." So saying she asked Birbal to remain at home for the next two days and instructed him not to go to the court.

On the third day Birbal's wife took with her a box of sweets and left for the palace. On reaching the palace she went up to the emperor and offered him the box of sweets.

"What is this for?" asked the emperor. "Do you have some good news to convey to me?". "Yes your majesty," replied Birbal's wife, "I have some good news to tell you. My husband Birbal gave birth to a baby yesterday. That is why I am offering these sweets to you."

"What!", exclaimed the emperor, "How can a man give birth to a baby?" "The same way as an ox can produce milk, your majesty," replied Birbal's wife.

The emperor was puzzled for a moment but soon realised the wisdom behind Birbal's wife's statement. He thanked her for pointing out his stupidity and asked her to apologize to Birbal for putting him in a tight spot.

Wisdom In
A Pitcher

The king of a neighbouring land once sent Emperor Akbar a letter through a messenger. The emperor opened the letter to find these strange words written in it: "Send me a pitcher of wisdom". Nobody could understand what it meant for it was a very strange request.

Emperor Akbar summoned Birbal and asked him, "What do you think this request means?" Birbal thought for a minute and then said: "Your majesty, this is indeed a very strange request. But I know how we can fulfil it." "Tell me how!", exclaimed the emperor excited

that Birbal seemed to have an answer for the strange request.

"Your majesty", replied Birbal, "Instead of telling you how, I will bring you the pitcher of wisdom if you give me a week's time." The emperor readily agreed to Birbal's request and sent word to the neighbouring land's king that he would send him the pitcher in a week's time.

Birbal soon bought an empty pitcher and went home. He then filled the pitcher with some soil and planted a few pumpkin seeds into the soil. He watered it regularly for a week and at the end of the week a pumpkin had grown to full size inside the pitcher! It was stuck inside the pitcher and would be impossible to take out since it was bigger than the mouth of the pitcher.

Birbal then took the pitcher to the court and asked the emperor to send it to the neighbouring king along with a letter.

The letter read, "Your Highness, here is the pitcher of wisdom but please make sure that you don't break the pitcher to take the wisdom out. Please send the empty pitcher back to us without damage."

The neighbouring land's king read the letter and immediately knew that he had been outwitted for how was it possible to take out the pumpkin without breaking the pitcher?

He then sent a note to Emperor Akbar apologising for having challenged him. The emperor thanked his lucky stars for having a wise minister like Birbal.

The Magic Sticks

A wealthy merchant once came to Emperor Akbar's court and said that he wanted a solution to a particular problem.

"Your majesty", said he, "I had kept a bag of gold coins in a cupboard in my house. I left my house for a few days as I had to go away on business. I made sure that I locked the cupboard before leaving. I returned last evening to find the cupboard open and my bag of gold missing. I have five servants working in my house and I am sure it is one of them who has taken it but I do not know how to find out which one is guilty of the crime."

Birbal heard the merchant's story. He consoled the merchant by saying that he knew how to find out who the guilty one was. He asked the merchant to send the five servants to him the next day.

The servants appeared in front of Birbal as scheduled. Birbal then handed each of them a stick and said, "I have given each of you a magic stick. Keep it with you and bring it back to me at the same time tomorrow. The guilty one's stick alone would have grown bigger by three inches." So saying he dismissed the servants.

The next day the servants came to the court bringing with them their sticks. Birbal measured each of the sticks and found one to be three inches shorter.

He pointed to the man with the shorter stick and said, "You are the guilty one. These sticks do not have any magic in them. They are ordinary sticks. I knew that the guilty one fearing that the stick might grow three inches bigger will cut three inches off it. That is exactly what you have done. Is that not why your stick is shorter than the others?"

The servant with the shorter stick immediately fell at Birbal's feet and asked for forgiveness. Birbal then asked him to return the merchant's bag of gold. The merchant was very impressed by Birbal's wisdom and showered him with gifts and lavish praises.

The Naughty Child

The morning session was in progress at Emperor Akbar's court but Birbal was nowhere to be seen.

The emperor waited patiently and soon Birbal arrived, late by an hour. Emperor Akbar asked Birbal the reason for his delay, to which Birbal replied, "Forgive me for arriving late your majesty. My daughter who is three years old has been crying the entire morning. It took me almost an hour to console her and make her stop crying."

The emperor found it ridiculous that Birbal had been detained by his

child's crying. "Why should it take you this long to console a child?" he asked Birbal.

"Your majesty," replied Birbal, "Children can be unreasonable at times. For you to understand this let me pretend to be a child and you can act as my father." The emperor agreed for he was curious to know what Birbal was upto.

Birbal then started wailing loudly. The emperor asked him what he wanted for which he replied, "I want a mango." So the emperor had his servant bring Birbal a mango.

On seeing the mango the child Birbal started to cry again. "I want the mango to be cut into pieces" he wailed. So the servant cut the mango into many pieces and offered it to Birbal.

Seeing the mango cut into pieces, Birbal started to cry even louder. "What is the matter now?" asked the emperor. "I want the same mango whole again and not cut into pieces," cried Birbal.

The emperor now understood why Birbal had said that children could be unreasonable and difficult to manage at times. He laughed at Birbal's clever play acting and agreed that it was not always an easy task to console a child.

The Clever Sadhu

It was Emperor Akbar's habit to go for a morning stroll in his beautiful gardens.

On one such walk he noticed that a few sadhus were sitting on a low wall that surrounded part of the palace gardens. "How dare they sit on the palace wall", he thought to himself.

The next morning he noticed the same sadhus sitting there and became quite furious. He sent word to the sadhus ordering them not to sit and rest on the palace wall again.

The sadhus were disheartened to hear this since it had become their favourite spot to take some rest. Meanwhile Birbal had come to hear of this and he thought that the emperor was being unjust and inhospitable to the poor sadhus. He decided to teach the emperor a lesson.

The next morning Birbal disguised as a sadhu went and sat on the low palace wall. The emperor while on his morning stroll noticed the lone sadhu sitting on the palace wall and called out to him, "Oh sadhu, did you not hear that I have ordered that nobody is allowed to sit on the palace walls?" Birbal, pretending to be the sadhu replied, "Your Highness, can you tell me who stayed in this palace before you?" "My father the great Humayun lived in this palace before me," replied the emperor. "And before that?" asked the sadhu. "Before that my grandfather Emperor Babar stayed here," replied the emperor. "And even before that?", asked the sadhu for which the emperor replied: "King Ibrahim Lodi lived here before my grandfather defeated him in a battle."

"So you see your highness, this palace has been like an inn where people come and stay till they leave and then someone else occupies it. The whole world is like an inn where people stay till they die and then go to their heavenly abode. Nothing is really permanent", replied the sadhu.

The emperor listened to the wise words of the sadhu and understood their true meaning. He then asked the sadhu's forgiveness and said that he would allow sadhus to sit on the palace walls.

Birbal then removed his disguise and the emperor was not surprised that it was Birbal again who had made him see the error of his ways.

The Loyal Birbal

Emperor Akbar and Birbal went for a walk one evening in the palace gardens. There were many vegetables, fruits and flowers growing in the garden.

The emperor was happy to notice that the gardens were really flourishing under the careful tending of the gardeners. As they walked on Emperor Akbar came across a sack full of carrots which had been plucked and washed and were ready to be taken to the royal kitchen.

The emperor said to Birbal, "I love carrots. They are so tasty and nutritious. Do you like them?" "Yes your majesty, I too love carrots for they do taste so good," replied Birbal.

A few days later the emperor invited Birbal to have lunch with him at the palace. Birbal agreed heartily for he was very hungry.

The cook had sliced some fresh carrots which was being served as part of the salad. Emperor Akbar suddenly wanted to test if Birbal really did like carrots as he had said the other day.

He told his servant not to serve him the sliced carrots saying, "I do not like carrots. They are tasteless and bring me no pleasure. What do you have to say Birbal?" Birbal replied instantly, "You are right your majesty, I too dislike carrots for they do not taste good."

"Ha!", thought Emperor Akbar, "I have trapped Birbal." "But Birbal," he said aloud, "Did you not tell me a few days ago that you loved carrots for they were so tasty?

Birbal stopped eating and said, "Your majesty, I am your servant and not the carrot's, servant. I thus owe my loyalty to you and not the carrots."

Hearing this the emperor was struck by how loyal and faithful his wise minister Birbal was to him. "No wonder that Birbal is my favourite minister," thought the emperor as he continued to eat.

Warmth Of The Light

Emperor Akbar was taking a walk one night in his palace gardens. He could see the river Yamuna from there, it was very cold and Akbar wondered, how cold the water from the Yamuna would be.

Suddenly, the emperor struck upon an idea. Next day in the court, Akbar said, "Anybody who stands upto his neck in the icy waters of the river Yamuna a whole night will be given two hundred gold coins."

There was no one who was willing to spend the whole night in the river. They were sure they would freeze to death.

But, there was a very poor man, he came to the palace and informed Akbar that he would stand neck deep in the Yamuna for a whole night. The poor man needed the money very badly.

On the given night, Akbar appointed two guards to keep watch. The poor man got into the freezing cold water till the water was upto his neck. No sooner had he got in than he started to shiver.

In the distance, the well lit towers of the palace were visible. The poor man took a look at the light in the towers and imagined their warmth. This made him feel better. Thus passed the whole night.

It was finally dawn, when Emperor Akbar came to the river, the poor man was still there and had won his reward.

Akbar was amazed and asked, "How did you manage it, tell me?" To which the poor man explained, "Your Highness, I imagined the warmth of the light in the palace towers and this kept me warm."

"What! So you have cheated. Go away, you do not deserve the reward," shouted Akbar. The poor man was shocked, but scared of the Emperor. Without a word, he left and went in search of the wise Birbal for help.

Birbal, listened to everything that the poor man told him and assured him that he would get his two hundred gold coins.

The next day, Emperor Akbar was to have an important meeting in court. Birbal was nowhere to be seen and the presence of Birbal was necessary.

Akbar sent two messengers to bring Birbal. The two messengers returned a little later and said, "O Emperor, Birbal is cooking some Pulav and will be coming shortly."

The whole court and the emperor waited for some more time. "How much longer do I have to wait," said Akbar annoyed, "Let us go and see, this wonderful dish that Birbal is cooking."

So, Akbar along with a few of his ministers went to Birbal's house. There they saw Birbal sitting beside a small fire with a pot tied-up high on a tree. Akbar was puzzled, "What are you doing, Birbal?" he asked. "I am making Pulav," replied Birbal. "You mean this small fire is going to heat the pot tied so far away. Are you making fun of me Birbal?" Akbar asked.

"Your Highness, just like the far away lamps in the palace towers provided warmth to a man in the freezing Yamuna, so will my small fire cook the Pulav," said Birbal.

Then, Akbar remembered what he had said to the poor man when he had sent him away and felt ashamed. He thanked Birbal for having showed him his mistake in not having rewarded the poor man.

Emperor Akbar, immediately sent for the poor man and gave him his two hundred gold coins and other gifts.

Birbal Is Banished

One day Emperor Akbar was very annoyed with Birbal and asked him to leave his kingdom.

But after Birbal had left, Akbar missed him greatly and sent many messengers in search of him. But all in vain. Birbal was nowhere to be found. As days went by, the emperor wanted the company of a wise man and Birbal had been the wisest.

One day, Akbar got some news that a very holy man had come to the city and he was wise too. Akbar sent for the holy man. When he came, Akbar said, "I have heard that you are holy and wise, I am looking for a Minister in court. If you can answer all questions to my satisfaction, I will make you a Minister."

"I am ready, Your Highness," said the holy man. The 'Nine Gems' in the emperor's court started the questioning.

"Who is man's best friend?" asked Todarmal. "His good sense," replied the holy man.

"A thing once lost cannot be recovered. What is it?" Asked Aziz Koka. "Life," came the reply.

The questions kept coming, another minister asked, "What travels faster than the wind." "Man's imagination," said the holy man.

The emperor himself decided to ask a few questions. He asked' "What does an emperor require to rule over a kingdom?" "Diplomacy."

"What is a king's greatest enemy?" asked Akbar again. "His selfishness."

Emperor Akbar was really impressed and said, "You are indeed a very wise man. I have just one more question to ask you. Can you bring back my best friend and advisor Birbal to my kingdom. The holy man did not say another word. He removed his false beard and wig. There before the whole court was Birbal himself.

Akbar laughed joyfully that it was none other than Birbal who had answered all the questions. He said, "Birbal! I should have known that only you could reply in this fashion," he said, "I am happy that you are back."

The Witness

Once during the rule of Emperor Akbar lived a wealthy merchant. His name was Dhansham. Dhansham was going on a pilgrimage and wanted to leave his wealth, a bag of gold coins with his close friend, Kedarnath.

The day Dhansham left on his pilgrimage, he handed over the bag of gold coins to Kedarnath and said, "Please look after my belongings, I will be back next month." Kedarnath agreed to keep the bag.

A month soon passed and Dhansham returned. He went over to

Kedarnath's house to get back his bag of valuables.

When Kedarnath saw Dhansham, he was very rude and said, "Why don't you come after three days I am really very busy now." Dhansham went again to Kedarnath's house after three days. Kedarnath was rude yet again and asked Dhansham to come a week later. This went on for almost two months.

Finally, Dhansham lost his patience and his temper and said, "Since you have no intention of returning my money, I will report you to Birbal, in the emperor Akbar's court."

So, the following day, Dhansham and Kedarnath went to present themselves before Birbal. After Birbal heard the story, he asked Dhansham,

"Where did you meet Kedarnath when you handed over the gold coins?" "It was in a farm under a mango tree," said Dhansham. "Ah, so we do have a witness, the mango tree," said Birbal.

Both, Dhanshan and Kedarnath looked puzzled. Birbal continued, "Dhansham, I want you to go up to the mango tree and tell the mango tree the whole story and also that I will be coming to meet it." Dhansham was really amazed by this order, but decided to do as he was told.

Kedarnath and Birbal waited for Dhansham's return. Two hours passed but there was no sign of Dhansham. "I wonder, what is taking Dhansham so long," said Birbal. "The farm is more than three miles from here and the mango tree is in the other end of the farm," said Kedarnath. Birbal looked at Kedarnath.

An hour later, Dhansham returned and said he had delivered the message to the mango tree. "The tree did not answer, just like I thought it would not," said Dhansham, a little annoyed with Birbal.

"Your tree has answered," said Birbal turning to Kedarnath, "If you did not take the money from Dhansham, how did you know where the farm was. Confess your crime."

Kedarnath, pleaded forgiveness from Birbal and returned the bag of gold coins to Dhansham.

How Many Pigeons

Once Emperor Akbar was walking in his palace gardens, when he saw scores of pigeons flying overhead. Akbar wondered, "How many pigeons are there in Agra?" He decided that he would pose this question to his courtiers.

So, after the court session was over. He looked at his courtiers and ministers and asked, "How many pigeons are there in Agra. Can anyone count them and tell me?"

Everyone was amused and puzzled with this strange question, but no one dared say anything wrong. Birbal got up from his seat and said, "Your Highness,

I will answer your question." "Yes, Birbal, you may," said Akbar, leaning forward to listen to Birbal's answer.

"Three hundred thousand, six hundred and twenty one is the exact number of pigeons in Agra, Your Highness," said Birbal. "How can you be so sure?" "What if I have all the pigeons in Agra caught and I find their number more or less than what you have just stated," said Akbar.

"If there are any more pigeons, it means the relatives of the pigeons in the city have come to visit them," said Birbal and continued "If there are any less pigeons then the pigeons in the city have gone to visit their relatives," said Birbal and sat down.

Akbar was pleased with Birbal's answer and applauded him.

Birbal, The Father

Emperor Akbar was as usual conducting the proceedings in court when a worried Birbal walked in.

"What is the matter Birbal?" Akbar asked. "I have just had a baby girl," said Birbal and continued, "Once a girl is born in our community, we have to start worrying about her marriage." To this Akbar consoled Birbal and said, "You have nothing to worry. I will take care of everything when the time comes."

Many years passed and Birbal's daughter was to be married. Emperor

Akbar made lavish arrangements and the guests were all very pleased and satisfied.

Next day when Birbal came to court, he was still a worried man. Akbar asked, "What is it now Birbal?" "O Emperor, the bridegroom's relatives have said that the bride's father is a miser," said Birbal. "How can that be when everything was so lavish," objected Akbar.

"They said that the pot containing gold coins at the exit had a narrow neck and not enough could be taken," said Birbal.

Akbar sighed and agreed that indeed a girl's father was not a happy man.

The Camel's Curved Neck

Emperor Akbar was to reward Birbal for a task Birbal had carried out for the Emperor. But Akbar had forgotten. Birbal had no idea how to remind Akbar.

One day, Akbar and Birbal were taking a walk when they came across a camel. Akbar wanted to have some fun, so he asked Birbal, "Tell me, Birbal, why is a camel's neck so curved."

Birbal replied, "O Emperor, it is said that the camel forgot to keep all its promises and God decided to punish it."

Suddenly, Emperor Akbar remembered his promise to Birbal. As soon as they returned to the palace, Akbar handed over the promised reward.

Birbal Frees
The Lion

Emperor Akbar was friendly with a number of kings and rulers. They were always exchanging puzzles and riddles and testing out each other's wit.

One day, the emperor received a strange gift from one of the kings. It was a lion in a cage. The lion looked very real and many of the courtiers were fooled into thinking so.

The gift was also accompanied with a letter. The letter read: "Remove the lion from the cage without moving it."

The Emperor was puzzled. Akbar looked at Birbal and asked, "Birbal, do you have any answer to this strange request?" "Please give me a day O Emperor," said Birbal

The next day, Birbal walked up to the cage and took a close look at the lion. He realised that it was made of wax. Birbal at once knew how to remove the lion from the cage. He asked one of the guards to heat an iron rod and bring it. The guard did as he was told. Birbal took the hot iron rod and pierced the lion with it. The wax started to melt and soon there was no sign of the lion.

Akbar and the whole court applauded Birbal. Birbal had once again proved his worth.

Divine Music

Tansen, one of the Nine Gems of Akbar's court was a great singer. Emperor Akbar was fond of good music.

Akbar came to know that Tansen's guru Swami Haridas was a better musician than Tansen. So, one day, Akbar summoned Tansen and said, "I hear that your guru Swami Haridas is an excellent singer, can you take me to him." Tansen agreed.

On the appointed day, Akbar, accompanied by Birbal along with Tansen went to meet Swami Haridas.

On reaching the Swami's ashram, Tansen presented himself in front of his guru and informed him of the purpose of his visit. Swami Haridas turned towards the Emperor and said, "O Emperor, I am sorry, I cannot sing when somebody commands me to. I have to be inspired."

Akbar was very disappointed and as they were returning, he asked Tansen, "Is there any way you can make the Swami sing?" "Yes, if I sing something wrongly the Swami is bound to correct me," said Tansen. Asking Akbar and Birbal to wait, Tansen went back to Swami Haridas.

Tansen sat in front of his guru and started singing a bhajan. Suddenly the Swami said, "No, No, it is not sung that way............it is like this.........." And Swami Haridas started to sing.

Emperor Akbar standing in the distance could hear the Swami sing and was enchanted with the melody. "Indeed Swami Haridas is a great singer but why cannot Tansen sing like his guru?" Asked Akbar to Birbal.

After a moment of thought Birbal said, "O Emperor, Tansen sings to please you, whereas Swami Haridas sings to please the gods. That is why the Swami's music is divine."

Akbar was satisfied with Birbal's reply and they returned back to the kingdom.

Clever Birbal

One day, a wise man, by the name of Veer Singh visited the court of Emperor Akbar. He was received and treated well. Veer Singh had a puzzle to ask of the Emperor and he challenged any one in the court to answer it.

Veer Singh started, "Once, three travellers wanted to rest at an Inn for the night. The Inn keeper had only a single room but with three cots. He charged them thirty gold coins. The three travellers paid it at once."

"Later, the Inn keeper realised that the actual charge for the room was only

twenty five gold coins and not thirty. He called his assistant and asked him to return the excess five gold coins to the three travellers."

"Now, the assistant was not as honest as the Inn keeper. He decided that since it was not easy dividing five gold coins, he might as well pocket two and give back three gold coins to the travellers. And that was what he did; he returned one gold coin to each of the three travellers."

Veer Singh continued, "Here is the problem; there were thirty coins; the assistant took two, and twenty seven coins were charged as rent. Twenty seven and two is twenty nine what happened to the other coin?"

All the courtiers looked puzzled. Birbal stood up and said, "It is actually quite simple. The three travellers paid thirty gold coins and received back three gold coins. Out of the twenty seven gold coins paid by the travellers two were taken by the assistant and the remaining is twenty five. There is really no missing coin."

Veer Singh and the whole court applauded Birbal. Veer Singh said, "Indeed Birbal you are right, it is just a tricky question."